Franklin's Bicycle Helmet

From an episode of the animated TV series *Franklin*
produced by Nelvana Limited, Neurones France s.a.r.l.
and Neurones Luxembourg S.A.

Based on the *Franklin* books by
Paulette Bourgeois and Brenda Clark.

TV tie-in adaptation written by Eva Moore
and illustrated by Sean Jeffrey, Mark Koren,
Alice Sinkner and Jelena Sisic.
TV script written by Nicola Barton.

Franklin

Franklin is a trade mark of Kids Can Press Ltd.
The character Franklin was created by Paulette Bourgeois and Brenda Clark.
Text copyright © 2000 by P.B. Creations Inc.
Illustrations copyright © 2000 by Brenda Clark Illustrator Inc.

Kids Can Press acknowledges the support of the Ontario Arts
Council, the Canada Council for the Arts and the Government of
Canada, through the BPIDP, for our publishing activity.

Kids Can Press Ltd.
29 Birch Avenue
Toronto, Ontario, Canada
M4V 1E2

Printed in Hong Kong by Wing King Tong Company Limited

CDN PA 00 0 9 8 7 6 5 4 3 2 1

Canadian Cataloguing in Publication Data

Franklin's bicycle helmet

(A Franklin TV storybook)
Based on characters created by Paulette Bourgeois and Brenda Clark.

ISBN 1-55074-730-4 (bound)   ISBN 1-55074-728-2 (pbk.)

I. Bourgeois, Paulette.   II. Clark, Brenda.   III. Series.

PS8550.F728 2000   jC813'.54   C99-932553-1
PZ7.F85924 2000

Kids Can Press is a Nelvana company

Franklin's Bicycle Helmet

Based on characters created by
Paulette Bourgeois and Brenda Clark

Kids Can Press

FRANKLIN could count by twos and tie his shoes. He could zip zippers and buckle buckles. But Franklin couldn't buckle up his bicycle helmet anymore. It was too small.

Franklin's mother took him to the store to get a new helmet. There were rows and rows of helmets to choose from. Franklin picked a silver and white one with a flashing red light on top.

"This is the one I want!" he said.

Franklin's mother checked the fit. It was just right.

"Are you sure you like this helmet?" she asked. "It's a little flashy."

"I think it's great," Franklin replied.

"Okay," said his mother. "If that's the one you want, that's the one we'll get."

Franklin did a happy dance.

That afternoon, Franklin practised his hand signals for the Bike Safety Rally.

"You're going to do fine tomorrow," said Franklin's father. "And I think Constable Raccoon will be impressed with your new helmet."

Franklin smiled proudly. "I can't wait to show it to my friends," he said.

The next morning, Franklin took his time
getting to the rally. He wanted all his friends to
be there when he arrived. He planned to surprise
everyone with his new helmet.

When he got to the schoolyard, Franklin hid behind some bushes. He could hear his friends talking.

"Have you seen those funny helmets with the flashing light on top?" asked Fox.

"I wouldn't wear one," said Beaver. "You'd look like a fire engine with one of those on your head."

Suddenly, Franklin wasn't so sure about his new helmet. He took it off and hung it on his handlebar.

Franklin left his bicycle behind the bushes
and walked over to his friends.

"Where's your bike?" asked Beaver.

"Um, I got a flat tire," Franklin fibbed.
"I can't ride in the rally," he added sadly.

"You can borrow my bike," offered Bear.
"My helmet too."

Franklin cheered up. "Okay, Bear!" he said.
"Thanks!"

Constable Raccoon blew his whistle. It was time for the rally to begin. The riders pushed their bikes towards the starting gate.

"What's that noise?" asked Fox.

"That's my bike," Rabbit said proudly. "I put cardboard in the wheel. Now my bike sounds like a motorcycle."

"Or like a piece of cardboard is stuck in your wheel," said Fox. He and Beaver laughed and ran ahead.

Rabbit looked embarrassed. "Maybe I should take the cardboard out," he said.

"I think it sounds neat," said Franklin.

"You do?" asked Rabbit. "I like it, too."

Rabbit thought for a moment, then made up his mind. "My bike is going to stay just the way it is!" he declared.

Constable Raccoon went over the safety rules. "And anyone who finishes the course without making a mistake will earn a shiny safety sticker," he announced.

Everyone was excited.

Fox was the first to get a sticker. Then Beaver and Rabbit earned their prizes. Bear did a perfect job, too.

Finally, it was Franklin's turn. He stepped forward with Bear's bike and helmet.

"Hold on, Franklin," said Constable Raccoon. "That helmet is too big for you. A helmet should fit snugly to give proper protection."

Franklin was disappointed.

"I'm sorry, Franklin," said Constable Raccoon, "but it wouldn't be safe for you to ride with that helmet. There will be another rally soon. I'll keep this sticker for you until then. Okay?"

Franklin nodded sadly. The rally was over.

Franklin was helping Constable Raccoon pack up when he noticed Rabbit behind the bushes. Rabbit had found his helmet!

Franklin raced over. "What are you doing?" he cried, snatching the helmet away.

Rabbit was surprised. "Is that yours?" he asked.

"Yes," Franklin admitted, "but I don't want anyone making fun of it."

"I won't make fun of it," said Rabbit. "I think it's amazing."

"You do?" said Franklin. He sighed. "So do I."

Franklin looked at his helmet for a minute. Then he put it on.

"Wait!" shouted Franklin as he ran to Constable Raccoon.

"Well now," said the constable. "Whose helmet is that?"

"It's mine," Franklin replied, looking at Fox and Beaver. "And I like it!"

"I like it, too," said Constable Raccoon. "It fits you properly, and you'll be seen from a mile away. Be safe! Be seen!"

Franklin took a deep breath. "Is it too late for me to try out for my safety sticker?"

Constable Raccoon smiled. "You're just in time," he answered.

Franklin finished the course perfectly and received his own shiny safety sticker. Then he rode home as fast as he could.

"I knew all my hand signals!" Franklin told his parents. "Look at the sticker I earned."

"Congratulations," said his mother.

"I knew you could do it," said his father. "Did everyone like your new helmet?"

Franklin grinned. "I don't know," he replied.
"But I sure do!"